Princess Truly

I Can Help!

WRITTEN BY
Kelly Greenawalt

ART BY
Amariah Rauscher

ACORN™
SCHOLASTIC INC.

To my seven favorites: Mama loves you
more than you will ever know. — KG

To Emma and Mikey. You will find yourselves in
chapter three on a hayride with Princess Truly. — AR

Text copyright © 2023 by Kelly Greenawalt
Illustrations copyright © 2023 by Amariah Rauscher

Library of Congress Cataloging-in-Publication Data
Names: Greenawalt, Kelly, author. | Rauscher, Amariah, illustrator.
Title: I can help! / written by Kelly Greenawalt ; art by Amariah Rauscher.
Description: First edition. | New York : Acorn/Scholastic Inc., 2023. |
Series: Princess Truly ; 8 | Audience: Ages 4–6. | Audience: Grades K–1. |
Summary: In three rhyming stories, Princess Truly helps her friend pack for her moving day,
cleans up the park with her pug, Sir Noodles,
and helps a farmer get his tractor keys back from a crow.
Identifiers: LCCN 2022034001 | ISBN 9781338883442 (paperback) | ISBN 9781338883459 (library binding)
Subjects: CYAC: Stories in rhyme. | Princesses—Fiction. | African Americans—Fiction. |
Superheroes—Fiction. | LCGFT: Stories in rhyme. | Picture books.
Classification: LCC PZ8.3.G7495 Ian 2023 (print) | DDC [E]—dc23
LC record available at https://lccn.loc.gov/2022034001

10 9 8 7 6 5 4 3 2 1   23 24 25 26 27

Printed in China   62

First edition, October 2023

Edited by Rachel Matson and Andy Lopez Soberano
Book design by Sarah Dvojack

Moving Day

I am Princess Truly.
This is Lizzie and May.

Our friend Eve is moving.

We're helping her today.

I unpin the poster.

Lizzie packs up the blocks.

Eve takes down her train set.

May puts toys in a box.

This is Eve's pet, Nacho.
We pack up her toys, too.

Nacho is not happy.
There's nothing fun to do!

Nacho has an idea.
She really wants to play.

Hide-and-seek is so fun.
Shh! Nacho sneaks away.

It's time for Eve to leave.
But she can't find Nacho!

The boxes are loaded.
The moving truck must go.

We will help Eve find her!

Lizzie looks over there.

May searches the closet.

I look under the stairs.

Hooray! I found Nacho.
Eve hugs her little mouse.

It's time to wave goodbye.
They drive to their new house.

The Stinky Park

We're helping at the park!
We rake leaves and we mow.

Next, we pull out the weeds
to help the flowers grow.

Sir Noodles wants to help.
Can he water the plants?

He grabs on to the hose.
But then he sees some ants.

Noodles does not like ants.
He jumps and runs away.

He bumps into a skunk,

who sends out stinky spray.

BARK!

The whole park is smelly.
Sir Noodles starts to bark.

I know just what to do.
I'll fix the stinky park!

I shake my magic curls.
They sparkle and they glow.

The tall trees start to shake.
The wind begins to blow.

My rainbow magic works!
It blows the stink away.

But Noodles still smells gross.
He needs a bath today.

I scrub and rinse my pup.
Noodles smells much better.

He shakes off the water.
He makes the plants wetter.

We are finished helping.
Now it is time to eat.

First we have a nice lunch.
And then we have a treat.

Super Helpful

Sir Noodles loves the farm.
There is so much to do.

We will pick some apples
and take a hayride, too.

I help my pup get on.
The tractor starts to go.

We pass lots of flowers.
We see a tall scarecrow.

I hop off at our stop.
Sir Noodles follows me.

We see yummy apples.
I pull them off the tree.

Now our basket is full.
We get back in the cart.

The farmer tries to go,
but the tractor won't start.

Look! That crow took the keys.
I know just what to do.

Time for rainbow magic.
I'll fly like the crow, too.

I fly up to her nest.

I have the keys. Hooray!

I am super helpful.
I always save the day.

About the Creators

Kelly Greenawalt is the mother of seven children. She lives in Texas with her family. Princess Truly was inspired by her daughters. Kelly loves helping others by volunteering in her community.

Amariah Rauscher loves helping, hide-and-seek, and hayrides. She can usually be found daydreaming about Princess Truly's next big adventure. Amariah lives in the New Orleans area of Louisiana with her family and furry friend Maggie.

Read these books featuring Princess Truly!

YOU CAN DRAW NACHO!

1 Draw Nacho's eyes, nose, and mouth.

2 Draw the outline of Nacho's face, her eyebrows, and her whiskers.

3 Add Nacho's body. Draw two ears and the top of her head!

4 Draw her arms.

5 Add Nacho's feet and tail.

6 Color in your drawing!

WHAT'S YOUR STORY?

Princess Truly helps out by fixing the stinky park.
Imagine that **you** are in the park with her!
How would you help Truly fix the park?
Write and draw your story!

scholastic.com/acorn